Never Give Nana's Bunny a Bath

Debbe Hughes Nelson

Never Give Nana's Bunny a Bath

Debbe Hughes Nelson

gatekeeper press™
TAMPA, FLORIDA

Library of Congress Control Number: 2021941283

ISBN (hardcover): 978-1-966373-69-8

ISBN (Paperback): 978-1-966373-68-1

eISBN : 978-1-966373-67-4

To my sons and grands, love you to the moon and back!

And for Kirsten, who loved animals.

Hi! My name is Nana Debbe and I have a bunny named Marne!
I give her sweet red strawberries as treats . . .

but I never, EVER give my bunny a bath!

I give her crunchy orange carrots . . .

but I never, ever,
EVER give my bunny a bath.

I give her brightly colored toys to play with . . .

but I never, ever, ever,
EVER give my bunny a bath!

I give Marne a litter box because she poops little brown balls of poop that look like your favorite cereal . . .

but I never, ever, ever, ever . . . EVER give my bunny a bath!

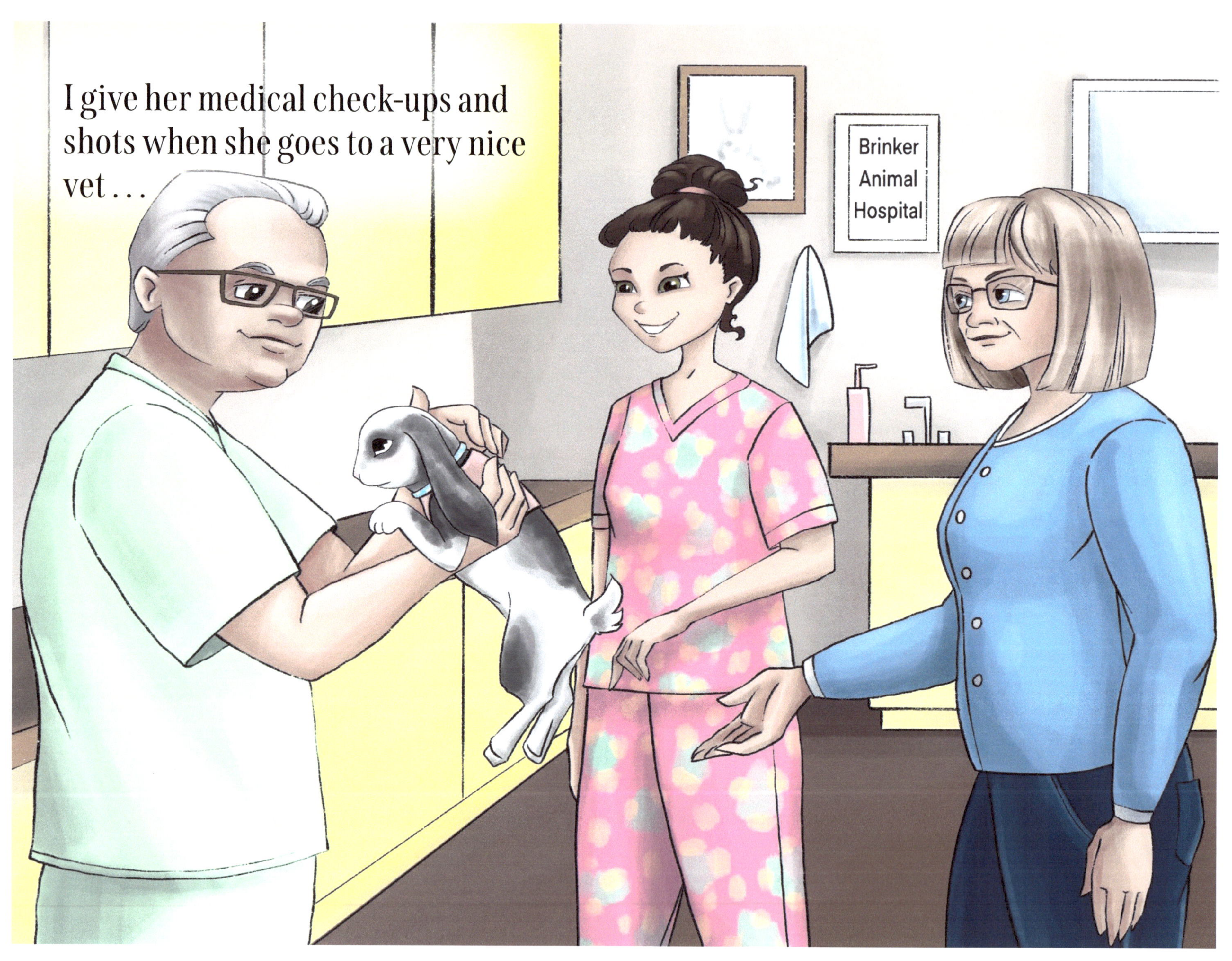

I give her medical check-ups and shots when she goes to a very nice vet . . .
Brinker
Animal
Hospital

but I never ever, ever,
ever, ever . . . EVER give
my bunny a bath!

I give her a den to hide in . . .

but I never, ever, ever,
ever, ever, ever . . . EVER
give my bunny a bath!

I give her a clean
and safe hutch to
sleep or play in . . .

but I never, ever,
ever, ever, ever,
ever, ever . . .
EVER give my
bunny a bath!

I give her a purple vest
to wear when she goes
out on the town . . .

but I never, ever, ever, ever, ever, ever, ever, ever . . . EVER give my bunny a bath!

I give her wild bike
rides in the basket
on my bike . . .

but I never ever, ever, ever,
ever, ever, ever, ever, ever . . .
EVER give my bunny a bath!

Best of all, I give her lots
and lots of loving snuggles .

but I never ever, ever, ever,
ever, ever, ever, ever, ever,
ever . . . EVER give my
bunny a bath!

WHY you ask? Because Marne is one smart bunny and gives herself a bath!

But wait …

Do you know how to give bunny kisses?

Scrunch up your nose and wiggle it! It's okay if you giggle because it tickles.

There, you can do it!

Now count the word "ever" together, then your child gets that many bunny kisses!

1, Just one and you're done!

2, You see two? Give your reader that many kisses, they want some too!

3, Three, you see? Your reader gives you kisses, they're free!

4, We have been counting forever you say? Is it your turn for more bunny kisses?

Now you can have fun looking for colors or shapes!

1. You can find the colors: red, orange, yellow, brown, blue, black, green, purple, teal, and pink.

2. Look for the shapes: octagons, triangles, rectangles, circles, ovals, squares, stars, pentagons, hexagons, and hearts.

Have fun counting, looking for colors, and finding shapes! I promise your child will still fall asleep. Now, off to dreamland with visions of bunnies and rainbows! Good night and sleep tight!

With love,

Nana Debbe

About the Author

Debbe Hughes Nelson lives in West Des Moines, Iowa, with her bunny, Marne Beatrix Nelson. She loves spending time with her family, is a proponent of early dyslexia diagnosis, supports the Animal Rescue League, and loves chocolate chip cookies. This is her first book in a planned series.